This book is dedicated to Mum, Dad, Nan, and Liz,
and to the friends in all our lives who encourage us to be more.

Who is your Seymour?

Special thanks to Maria

Splat Says Thank You
Copyright © 2012 by Rob Scotton
All rights reserved. Printed in the United States of America.
No part of this book may be used or reproduced in any manner whatsoever without
written permission except in the case of brief quotations embodied in critical articles
and reviews. For information address HarperCollins Children's Books, a division of
HarperCollins Publishers, 10 East 53rd Street, New York, NY 10022.
www.harpercollinschildrens.com
Library of Congress Cataloging-in-Publication Data is available.
ISBN 978-0-06-197874-6
The artist used sketchbook and pencil, Corel Painter, Adobe Photoshop,
and endless coffee to create the digital art for this book.
Typography by Jeanne L. Hogle
12 13 14 15 16   LP   10 9 8 7 6 5 4 3 2 1
❖
First Edition

Splat Says Thank You

For Seymour

by Splat

Rob Scotton

HARPER
An Imprint of HarperCollinsPublishers

Splat was worried that Seymour hadn't smiled all day.

He was covered in spots and not feeling well.

This isn't right, thought Splat. *How can I make Seymour smile?*

Splat pulled a book from a drawer and showed it to Seymour.

"I made it for you," Splat said. "I call it a Friendship Book."

Splat opened the book. It began quite simply.

For Seymour, the best mouse I know.

Seymour sneezed.
Splat turned the page and began to read aloud.

"When I was scared to try out for the school play, you encouraged me to do it anyway," said Splat.

"Thank you!"

"And when I laughed so hard at Plank that I forgot my lines . . ."

"... you helped me to remember them.

"Thank you!"

Splat looked at Seymour and thought that he was just about to smile. But he sneezed instead.

Achoo. . . .

Splat read on.

"When I broke my mom's favorite ornament,
you fixed it for me," said Splat.

"Except somehow, Mom noticed and I had to have a bath and go to bed early.

"Thank you, anyway."

"When I had my bath and got my toe stuck, you knew what to do.

"Thank you!"

"And when I went to bed early, you sneaked me a flashlight so I could read my book," said Splat.

"Thank you!"

"When I overslept the next morning, you woke me up
so that I wasn't late for school," said Splat.

"Thank you!"

"When I borrowed my brother's kite and we played for hours, you made it so much fun.

"Thank you!" said Splat.

"Then when I climbed a tree to rescue my brother's kite and got stuck . . . ."

"... you rescued me," said Splat.

"Thank you!"

Splat looked at Seymour and thought that he had to smile this time, but he hiccuped instead!
Splat read on.

"When I pretended I was speeding through space in my rocket ship, about to be the first cat on the moon . . .

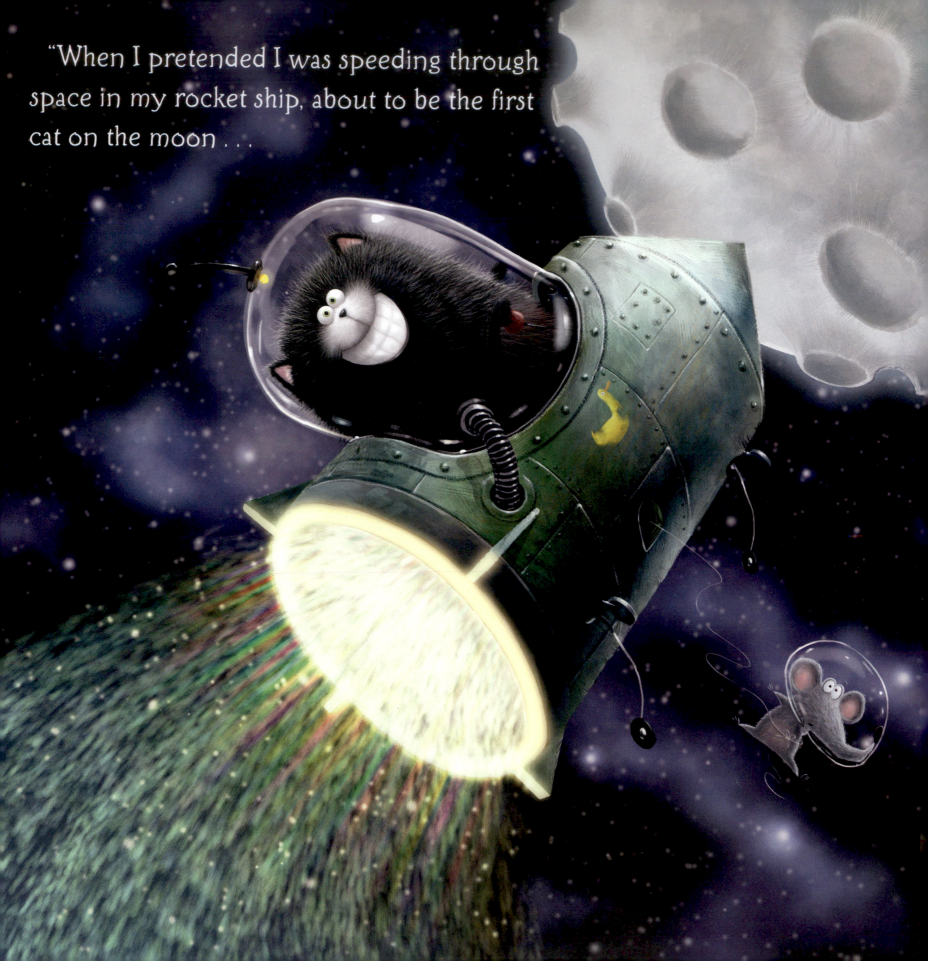

...and Spike passed me in a faster rocket ship and tried to become the first cat on the moon instead, you told me Space Cats never give up..."

"...so I didn't," continued Splat.

"Thank you!"

Splat looked at Seymour and thought that Seymour
was sure to smile this time.
But Seymour scratched a tickly ear instead . . .

scratch . . .

. . . so Splat read some more.

"When I told you my biggest secret,

you didn't tell anyone else.

"Thank you!"

"And when Spike gave Kitten a bigger Valentine card than the one I gave her,

you knew how to make me feel better.

"Thank you."

"When Little Sis was covered in spots and not feeling well, you made her smile," said Splat.

"Thank you!"

"And when I was covered in spots and not feeling well, you made me smile.

"Thank you!"

"You are my smallest friend and my biggest," he added.

"And I just want to say . . ."

"Thank you!"